This book is given with love

_____

_____

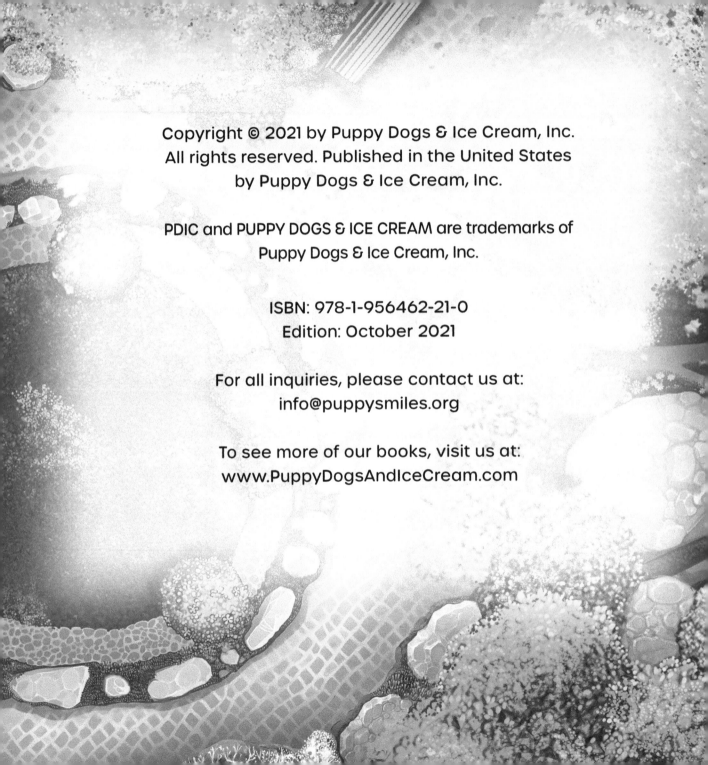

ISBN: 978-1-956462-21-0
Edition: October 2021

For all inquiries, please contact us at:
info@puppysmiles.org

To see more of our books, visit us at:
www.PuppyDogsAndIceCream.com

Seasons of Life
Our Walk with Christ

Written by **Marilee Joy Mayfield**

Illustrated by **Max Dolynny**

A little girl held hands with her older brother,
And their father held hands along with their mother.
It was late afternoon as they walked through the park,
And the winter sky was now turning dark.

Their mom said, "What a beautiful day it is for this walk."
Their dad added, "Yes, it helps us to think, pray, and talk."
The boy said, "Look! There's a scene of the nativity."
The girl asked, "Can we walk closer? I want to see!"

As they got near to the scene, they began to realize
That the statues in the stable were almost life-size.
They stood there in awe at the scene in the snow,
The Christmas lights gave it a heavenly glow.

And above the scene was the Christmas star,
On that holy night it was seen from afar.
Three wise men traveled by its bright light
To bring precious gifts to the stable at night.

The girl exclaimed, "It's beautiful! And it's such a loving scene,
With Joseph, Mary, and baby Jesus in-between."
"Yes," said their mom. "They were glad to find a place for the night.
There weren't rooms for them to stay in, though it doesn't seem right."

The boy asked, "What do you think God was trying to say
With Jesus being born in such a humble way?"
Their dad replied, "You're asking a question that is very wise.
I think God wanted to see through human eyes."

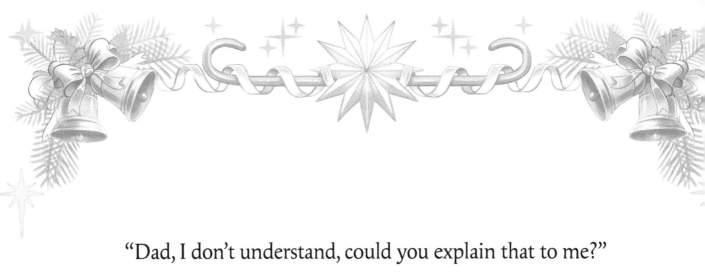

"Dad, I don't understand, could you explain that to me?"
"I'll try," said Dad, "maybe it'll be easier with a story.
When you were born, the world felt wonderful and new.
The day you opened your eyes, I saw the world from your view."

"I think I understand," said the boy, not sure if he was right,
"Through His Son's eyes, God saw the world with human sight.
Because Jesus became mortal and lived among us here...
God felt our feelings of love, happiness, and fear."

"Yes," continued their mom, "But there's something more,
Although I never quite thought of it this way before.
Jesus was the Word made flesh, a gift from above,
So that we could understand the nature of God's love."

"God must have loved us a lot," the girl started to say,
"To let His Son sleep in a manger filled with hay."
Their dad smiled, "Let's give thanks that Christ lived on Earth,
And that God sent His only Son to let us know our worth."

The girl said, "When we go home and place the star on our tree,
It's going to have a new meaning that I didn't see.
Just like the star guided the wise men to the nativity,
Our star guides our hearts for all that Christmas can be."

"Yes," said their mom, "It's easy to get distracted during this season,
But we should never forget that Jesus is the reason!
We're celebrating and commemorating the day of His birth,
For He saved us from sin when He came to Earth."

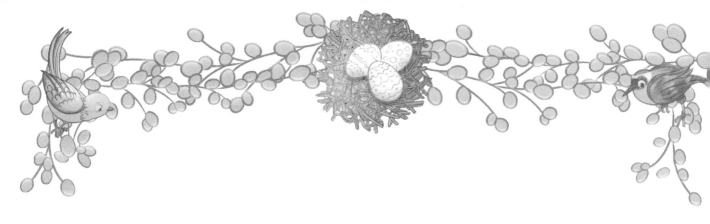

A few months went by and they were back at the park,
And they heard the song of a distant meadowlark.
Spring was in flower and green buds were on the trees.
The sky was bright blue, and there was a light, cool breeze.

As they walked, new plants were springing up from the ground.
There were tiny, green shoots pushing up all around.
Their mom said, "This reminds me of a very special story…
A parable told by Jesus about receiving heaven's glory."

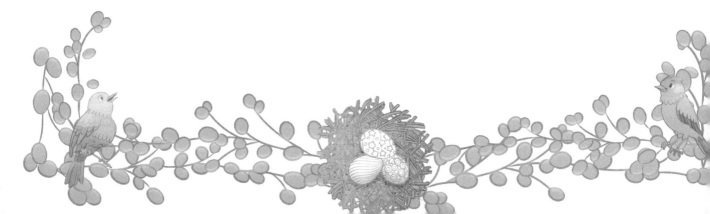

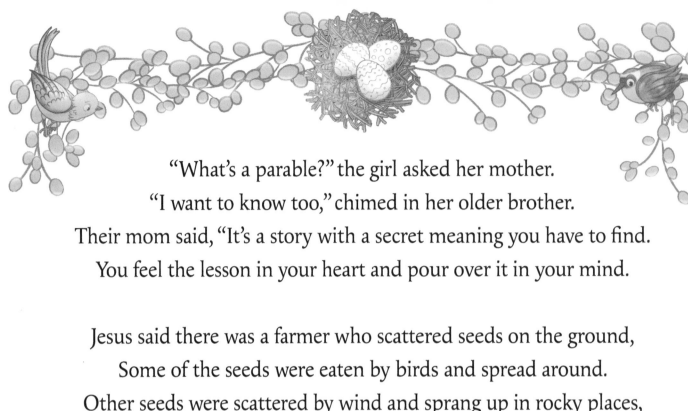

"What's a parable?" the girl asked her mother.
"I want to know too," chimed in her older brother.
Their mom said, "It's a story with a secret meaning you have to find.
You feel the lesson in your heart and pour over it in your mind.

Jesus said there was a farmer who scattered seeds on the ground,
Some of the seeds were eaten by birds and spread around.
Other seeds were scattered by wind and sprang up in rocky places,
But there wasn't much rich soil or that many fertile spaces."

Their mom paused to ask, "Do you think those seeds grew?"
"No," said the girl and the boy agreed too.
"Correct, there wasn't enough soil to nourish those seeds.
Some were scorched by sun and some choked by weeds."

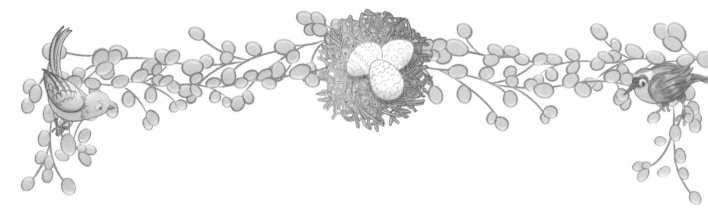

"So what happened?" asked the boy. "Did any plants grow?"
Their mom said, "If you think about it, you might already know.
Some fell on good soil where they grew and didn't stop,
And produced a hundred times over the farmer's first crop!"

Their dad asked, "What do you think of that story you two?
If God is the farmer, which type of soil are you?"
The boy answered, "I want to be the type where plants grow and grow!"
The girl said, "I want to be the soil with beautiful flowers to show!"

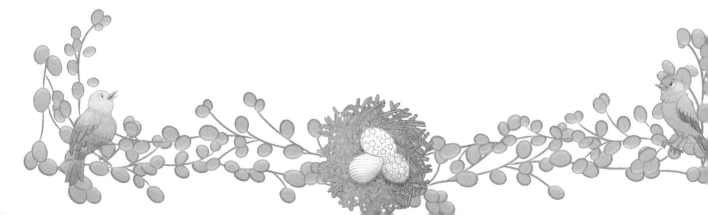

The girl asked, "When did Jesus tell this parable aloud?"
Their mom answered, "As an adult, speaking to a big crowd.
He knew He was the Son of God at a very early age,
And that He'd spread God's Word upon life's stage."

Their dad nodded, "There's another story when Jesus wasn't very old,
He was traveling with His parents and did something bold.
They headed back home after Passover took place,
When His parents noticed Jesus was gone without a trace."

"Oh, no! Was Jesus lost?" the girl asked, "Where did He go?"
"I don't remember this story," said the boy, "I want to know."
Their dad said, "They found Jesus down by the temple stairs
As He talked with wise men. God had answered their prayers."

"That's amazing!" said the girl, "Were His parents mad?"
Their dad said, "Yes, but He was safe, so they were also glad."
The boy asked, "What did Jesus say to them when He was found?"
Their mom said, "He didn't know why they were looking around.

Jesus asked his parents, 'Why were you searching for me?
Don't you know my Father's house is where I'm supposed to be?'
He was only twelve years old, but He already knew,
Who He was and everything He was destined to do."

Their mom continued, "Jesus' parents couldn't fully understand,
The seasons of His life that were already planned.
He was their Son on Earth, but it was also true...
That He was divine, since He was God's Son too."

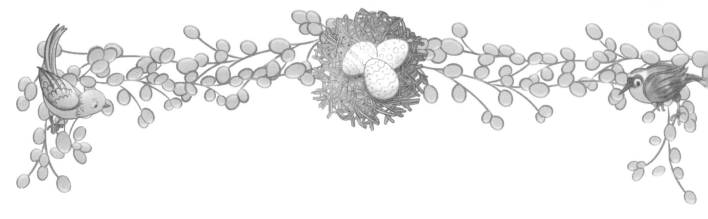

The children were listening as they continued to walk.
They loved to hear about Christ's life from their parents' talk.
Suddenly, they stumbled on something hidden in the field.
It was a bird's nest! The children smiled and kneeled.

"How pretty!" the girl said. "Look at the speckled eggs we found."
"It's a meadowlark's eggs," their mom nodded. "They nest on the ground."
"It reminds me of an Easter basket," the boy said, "and the eggs we hide.
I wonder when the baby birds will hatch and come outside."

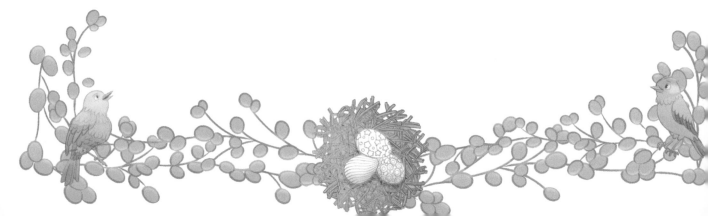

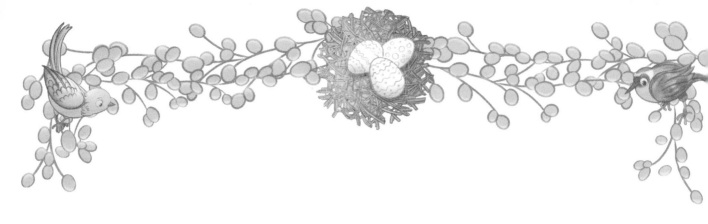

Their mom said, "Easter is just a few weeks away, and then we'll celebrate.
Do you happen to know why it is such an important date?"
Their dad answered, "Jesus was born, lived, and died for us on the cross.
The disciples mourned His passing. His death was a terrible loss."

"I know what happened next," the girl said, "He rose from the dead,
And they found the cloth that was wrapped around His head."
"And an angel said that Jesus wasn't there anymore.
He had risen," said the boy, "He's the Lord we adore!"

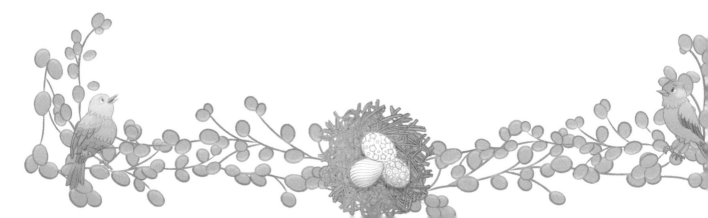

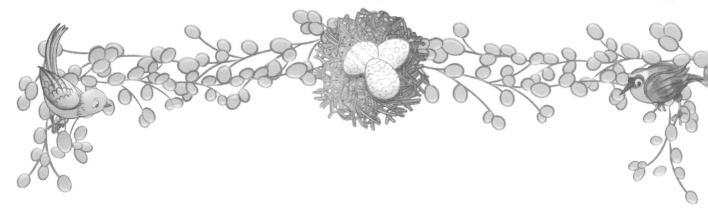

The girl asked, "What do eggs have to do with Easter though?"
The boy spoke up, "I think I understand, but I'm not sure I know."
Their dad said, "A bird escapes its shell and raises its head."
Their mom continued, "Like Jesus left His tomb and rose from the dead."

"I get it now," said the girl, "And Jesus is here with us now, isn't He?"
"Yes," said their mom, "He's by our side, wherever we may be...
Just like God, the Holy Spirit, and the love that they show."
"And if you trust in Him," their dad added, "Your faith will grow."

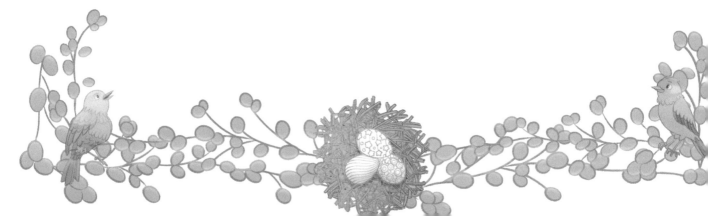

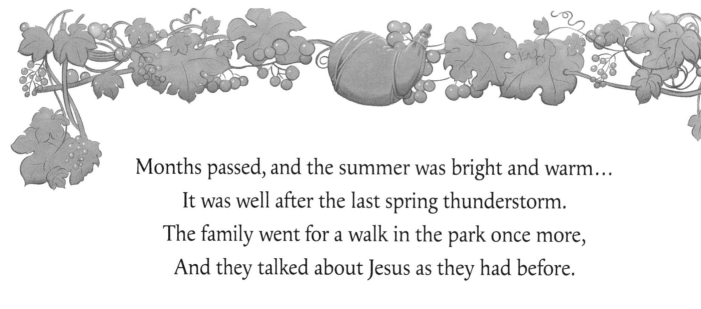

Months passed, and the summer was bright and warm…
It was well after the last spring thunderstorm.
The family went for a walk in the park once more,
And they talked about Jesus as they had before.

The girl asked, "Dad, is there another story that Jesus told?"
"I will tell you my favorite," said their dad. "It never gets old."
The children were quiet as they walked along,
And their dad's voice was loud, steady, and strong.

"Jesus said that a traveler was making a long journey alone…
When bandits robbed and beat him, far from his home.
One man ignored him by simply stepping aside.
A second man didn't stop, and even quickened his stride."

"Finally, a third man took pity on the traveler's soul.
He bandaged his wounds to help him feel whole.
He put the traveler on his donkey as he looked for a place to stay,
And paid for him to be taken care of that day."

Their dad then asked, "Who was a good neighbor to this traveling man?
Who was the person that followed Christ's plan?"
"The third man," said the girl, "It was kind to do that for someone."
"Yes!" said the boy, "And that's also what Jesus would have done."

The girl smiled, "I love Jesus' stories. Can you tell us another?"
"I'd like to hear another one too!" said her brother.
Their dad took a mustard seed out of his pocket to show.
"I carry this seed with me wherever I go...

Jesus compared this to God's Kingdom. It's the tiniest seed of all,
But it grows up to be a tree that's actually big and tall.
And birds go into its branches to both sleep and nest
Because it is the tree that shelters them best."

Their mom added, "I have another mustard seed parable for you...
Jesus said there isn't a limit to what we can do.
If we have faith as big as this tiny seed in Dad's hand,
Then we can achieve everything for us that God has planned."

"Is that why you carry it, Dad?" The boy wanted to know.
"Yes, so I remind myself that my faith can grow."
The children were happy as they walked hand in hand,
And as the seasons passed, they grew to understand.

Soon it was fall and the trees were colored brown, red, and gold,
And as they walked in the park, they picked up leaves to hold.
The children jumped in the colorful piles on the ground.
They just loved to hear that leaf-crunching sound.

Their dad then reflected, "We have seasons too, starting with birth...
We open our eyes and are greeted by Earth.
As we grow, we learn more about ourselves through work and play,
And we become different and stronger with each passing day.

Then, as adults, we become the people we're meant to be,
We achieve goals with talents that everyone can see.
The years go by and our bodies don't last...
And soon, our earthly life is in the past."

Their mom said, "Yes, this is harvest time. It's the time of year...
When we should think about what we truly hold dear.
Jesus said that when a single kernel of golden wheat dies,
It goes into the soil and then multiplies."

"What does that mean, Mom?" The boy wanted to know.
"It means that whatever we value in life shall grow."
She said, "We must not covet our Earthly things
In order to give our souls their heavenly wings."

As they walked, the boy said, "The park looks different every season."
"Yes," said the girl, "I think that the trees are the main reason.
It's amazing how they change throughout the year.
They have transformed every time that we're here.

In winter, they lose their leaves and become skeletons against the sky.
In spring, new buds pop out, and the trees grow full and high.
In summer, they need nourishing water to remain their new size,
And in fall, they carry crowns of colors to show that they're wise."

So, the family held hands as they looked at the sky,
While a flock of wild geese went flying by.
It was a moment to remember, give thanks, and pray
Surrounded by the beauty of God's perfect autumn day.

"Mom, do you think that heaven is as beautiful as these trees?"
Asked the girl looking in wonder at the colorful leaves.
"Yes, heaven is beautiful, like all the seasons, not just fall,
But the most beautiful season of life is the love God has for us all."

Claim Your FREE Gift

 Visit

PDICBooks.com/Gift

Thank you for purchasing "Seasons of Life," and welcome to the Puppy Dogs & Ice Cream family.

We're certain you're going to love the little gift we've prepared for you at the website above.

CPSIA information can be obtained
at www.ICGtesting.com
Printed in the USA
BVHW021006211121
622164BV00015B/1272